The first creature we met, I believe was a bird.
Said, "My name is Ethel"....Now that was absurd!
She was part of the Emu welcoming committee,
To say a big Emu hello to the folk from the city.

Ethel gulped, "I am your guide for the day,
To show you our skills and the games we all play.
The animals are ready for the Grand Bilby Show.
A most splendid event now…. Didn't you know?"

Off to the bush, there was no time to waste,
With Daddy and John, Katie, Mathew and Grace.
And Mummy and Nettie who were quite slow to walk.
They needed to learn how to walk while they talk!

My Aussie Bush Adventure Belongs to:

_____

Look out for Nelly The Wombat
.....she likes to hide!

For Harry & for Katie, Mathew & Grace
Thanks Mac & Pa

Harry loves 'writing' letters to his Grandparents known as Mac and Pa.
'My Aussie Bush Adventure' is another letter Harry wishes to
share with you as part of the 'My Adventure Series'.

This series has been created to promote Australia.
More important however, it is to encourage children to have a sense of fun and
imagination. It is also the hope of the author that children will be encouraged
to write a letter…and post it!

Look out for further books in this series:
My Melbourne Adventure
My Phillip Island Adventure
My Warburton Adventure
My Mornington Peninsula Adventure
My Sydney Adventure
My Tassie Adventure

Published by Rothwell Publishing
9 Clarke Avenue, Warburton, Victoria, Australia, 3799
Tele: +61   03 5966 5628
Email: rothwellpublishing@bigpond.com
www.rothwellpublishing.com

First Published 2005
Reprinted 2006
Text copyright * Jo Rothwell 2005
Illustrations copyright * Bryce Rothwell 2005

National Library of Australia
Cataloguing-in-Publication data:

Rothwell, Jo, 1962-
My Aussie Bush Adventure.

For children
ISBN 0 9757230 1 4

1. Animals – Australia – Juvenile fiction.
I. Rothwell, Bryce, 1966- . II. Title.

A823.4

Typeset by Artastic Images
Printed in China by Everbest Printing Co Ltd

My Aussie Bush
Adventure

Jo Rothwell
Illustrated by
Bryce Rothwell

Rothwell
Publishing

Dear Mac and Pa,
I hope you are well.
I am writing to you with so much to tell.
This is what happened to Nelly and me,
In the Australian bush.......read on and you'll see.

So we followed Ethel, who took us to see,
A Koala bungy jumping from a Eucalyptus tree.
I thought this was quite an odd thing to do,
But Ethel explained it was leaves he pursued.

"He retrieves the leaves fallen down from his tree,
And returns to his branch as quick as could be."
Unfortunately whilst we were watching him jump,
The rope stretched too far, which caused quite a bump.

The Koala landed on an Echidna's head,
And he screamed out loudly; I can't repeat what he said.
But he seemed okay after his prickly ordeal,
Because he climbed up the tree to finish his meal.

Ethel then showed us the Birds of Prey,
Where the Wedge-tailed Eagles revealed their display.
They were soaring about just near where I sat,
When an eagle flew low and got caught in my hat.

Off came my hat and with it she flew,
To cover her head with my hat that was blue.

We then met Wombats, George and Bert.
They wore flannel shirts and were digging in dirt.

They couldn't stop to chat because they had no time to spare.
They were racing other Wombats who were chomping wooden chairs.

"It is now time," said Ethel, "to cover your ears,
As this mob will go wild with their clapping and cheers.
The Dingo Duet are about to begin.
Together they will howl and yowl and sing."

Ethel was right..... the noise was so loud,
The screeching was deafening from fans in the crowd.
I thought that Dingoes only howled at the moon,
Not here at a show harmonizing at noon!

We were now really hungry and it was time to eat.
An Ibis looked eager to find us a seat.
He then began to call all his mates,
To walk through our picnic, our cups and our plates.

Daddy and John didn't like this invasion,
So told the Ibis with the utmost persuasion.
That this was no good, it was in fact rude,
To invite all his mates to eat all our food.

It was now time to view the Platypus Five,
Who perform an incredible synchronized dive.
They had obviously taken some time to perfect,
This dive from the board… all together they leapt.

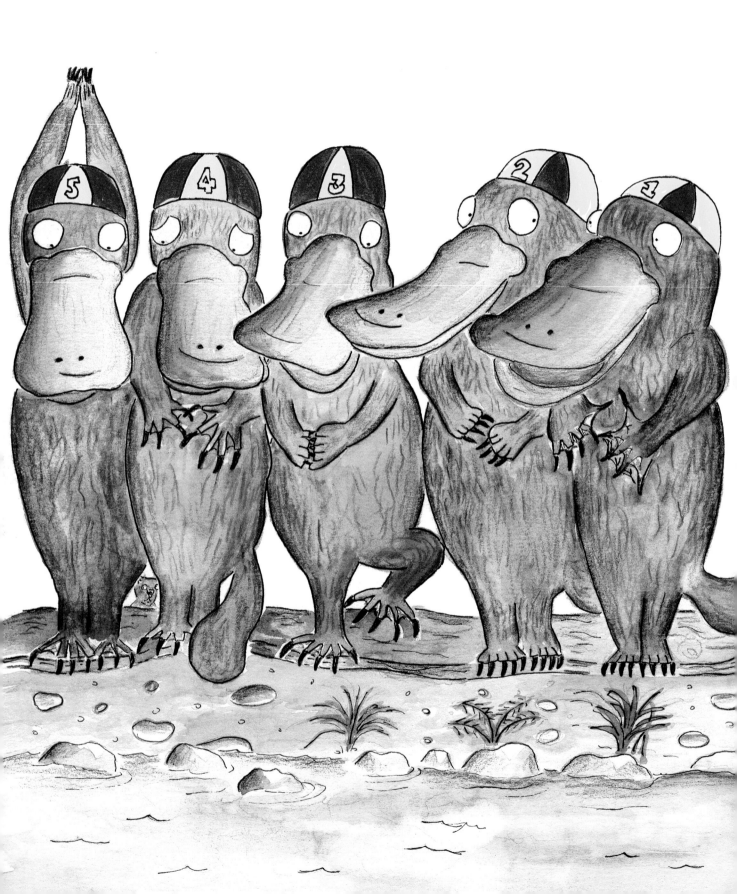

Unfortunately whilst they were taking this leap,
Platypus Three tripped over his feet.
He then grabbed hold of Platypus Four,
And fell into the water with cries of

"Encore".

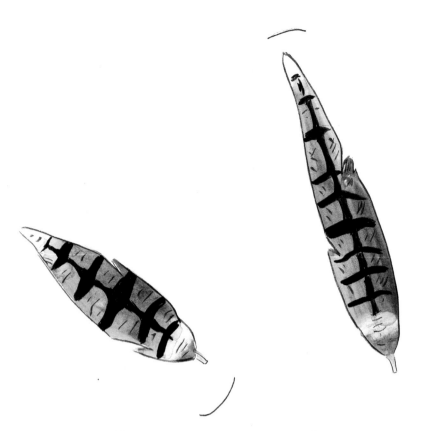

Well Mac and Pa, we next had a look,
At Kookaburras laughing until their tail feathers shook.
We all laughed as well and then fell on the floor.
I giggled so much that my sides are still sore.

We then went to look at the Kangaroos,
Who were lying about pretending to snooze.
But all of a sudden Big Red jumped up high,
And declared it was time to leap to the sky.

The Roos woke up for the Kanga Cup.
Open to anyone trying their luck
So I started off running as fast as I could,
And then stretched my legs as far as they would….

It wasn't too long before I fell from the sky,
I didn't win the cup, but I really did try…..

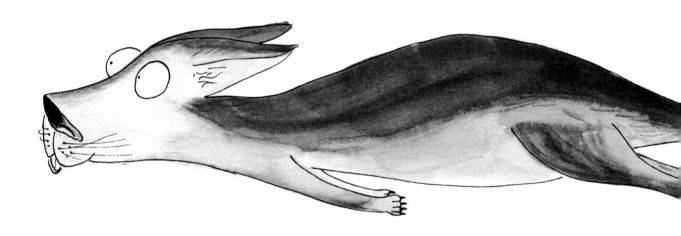

It was Big Red himself who had the longest leap,
And you could see why by the size of his feet.
He jumped so far you would think he had wings,
But he didn't need wings when his feet had Roo springs.

The next performance was quite a surprise,
When a Brolga tap danced in front of our eyes.
It was Lola the Brolga who danced loud and proud,
With music provided from birds in the crowd.

There were Parrots and Galahs and Rosellas as well,
And I think a Lyrebird, although it was hard to tell.
Because the Lyrebird can mimic any number of sounds.
They take time to learn all their noisy surrounds.

Ethel then said "I will now say goodbye,
Because the time has come to soar in the sky."
Daddy said her wings were too small to fly,
"I fly a red plane!" was Ethel's reply.

She was the very last act at the Grand Bilby Fair,
And her skills were amazing as she spun in the air.

I think that the bush is a great place to be,
With Possums and Lizards and Iron Bark Trees.
There were Frogs and Goannas and small Potoroos,
Paper Bark Trees and Black Cockatoos.

So our Aussie Bush adventure had come to an end,
And so is this letter I'll soon have to send.
I know we'll return, we will often come back,
And you can come too, Pa and Mac

Love Always,
Harry xxx

P.T.O.

Wombat:

Well I just love Wombats, especially Nelly, my own cuddly one. I'm not sure which type of Wombat Nelly is because she could be a Common or a Hairy Nosed one. She is probably Hairy Nosed because she has whiskers on her face and she is certainly *not* common. Daddy says that Wombats are called the 'bulldozers of the bush'. That is because they burrow and dig stuff. I have a toy bulldozer that I play with in my sandpit.

Emu:

The Emu is a bird except that it doesn't fly. So I guess it is lucky that it has feathers or we would probably get it confused with an animal that wasn't a bird. I think the Emu makes a really cool gulping sound and I have been practicing this every day. Mummy said that the Emu is on the Australian Coat of Arms along with the Kangaroo. This is because they both cannot walk backwards and Australia is advancing. All this is way too much for me because I didn't even know that Emus or Kangaroos wore coats.

Platypus:

Well Mac and Pa, I think the Platypus are wonderful creatures. Apparently they are really unusual because they are a mammal that lay eggs. I have chooks that lay eggs too. But my chooks don't swim like them or have feet like them or have fur like them and their beak is different. Actually my chooks really don't look like a Platypus at all. If I get up really early in the morning I might see a Platypus in our Yarra River.

Bilby:

Now these are cute but a bit weird looking. They have a body that looks like a Kangaroo, but have these really big unfortunate ears. Mummy said that instead of the Easter Bunny, we have the Easter Bilby. I reckon any creature that wants to give me chocolate is okay.

Koala:

Now here is a lovely cuddly creature. They need Eucalyptus trees to live in and eat the leaves. Did you know that a Koala can sleep for 19 hours a day? Wow! If I slept that long I wouldn't have any time to play with my trains. Daddy said that they don't need water because they get enough from the leaves. I tried sucking water from a leaf but it just tasted like dirt.

Ibis:

Now this bird is really scraggy looking and, no offence but I think they are a bit ugly. They seem to show up when food is about and they try and eat it up.

Wedge-tailed Eagle:

Now this is a bird that can fly! This bird is huge and has feathers on its legs that make it look kind of funny when it walks. Daddy says it is a bird of prey. This doesn't mean it goes to church. Daddy said that birds like pelicans and owls are also birds of prey. He said that sometimes people think that they eat sheep and other big animals, but this isn't true, they only munch on these animals when they are already kaput. They have really big nests too, almost as big as my sandpit. Daddy also told me that they had a wedge shaped tail and that is why they are called Wedge-tailed Eagles. I had already figured that out…but I let Daddy think he had told me something new anyway.

Brolga:

Yet another bird, but this one really dances. It has long legs and prances and dances. I think that if I had long legs like a Brolga I would play basketball.

Kookaburra:

These birds are really cool because they make the best noise. I can do the Kookaburra laugh just like them. One did annoy me once though, because I was running and then fell down and then a Kookaburra laughed at me and I thought that was a bit rude. They can see lots of worms and lizards and snakes and stuff and fly down from a tree and eat them.

Dingo:

These look like dogs but they don't bark, they howl. Mummy said that I used to howl when I was a baby, but now I don't. I love our dogs and love taking them for a walk.

Kangaroo:

Mummy said that when the European explorers first saw these hopping animals they asked a native Australian what they were called. He said "kangaroo" which means "I don't understand" your question. The explorers got confused and thought he was saying the animal's name. Mummy said that this was probably not the only time the explorers got confused. My Daddy and John and Annette all barrack for the Kangaroos footy side and that's something I don't understand. ….Go Blues.

Galah:

I heard my Daddy once call someone a Galah. I think Galahs are grey and pink and squawk a lot.

Lyrebird:

I seem to be telling you a lot about birds in this section of the book Mac and Pa. Okay, well I thought that the Lyrebird didn't tell the truth, but apparently I was confused….again, because Mummy told me that their tail feathers look like a lyre. Apparently a lyre is an old days musical instrument. I think my explanation is better.

Bush:

The bush is really anywhere that there are trees and animals. I think it is quite obvious what bush is. I think you are really lucky if you have bush where you live. You really should look after the bush because it is important to everything.